# THE LOLLIPOP TRILOGY

Book 1
## Lollipopman: Hero of the Highway

Written and Illustrated by
Philip Sheppard

www.lollipopman.co.uk

A Baa Code Book

25 Main Street
Gristhorpe
Filey
YO14 9PP

Copyright © Philip Sheppard 2005

ISBN 978-0-9551171-0-7

Printed in England by Crystal CP (tel: 020 8801 1733) using MetalFX Technology
(www.metal-fx.com) and ink from Wolstenholme International (www.wolstenholme-
int.com) and Stehlin Hostag (www.stehlin.co.uk).

First published in Great Britain by Baa Code Books in 2005

# Supporting

Profits from this book go to Brake – the road safety charity

Lollipopman supports the THINK! campaign

# Sponsors

020 8801 1733

www.metal-fx.com          www.wolstenholme-int.com

Special thanks to Alan Bowman for the spark of an idea & giving Lollipopman a theme tune.

With thanks to Aimee Bowen of Brake & Alice Evans from the Department for Transport; Mark at Crystal for his generosity; Nicky & Lee for their time & expertise; Andrew & the MetalFX team; Jean, Michelle & the folks at Wolstenholme; Fiona for lending her golden tonsils & Mike from Big3 for recording them; Dave from Stehlin Hostag; & to all friends and family for their help,  encouragement and support.

You are ace.

Pops, the Middletown lollipop man, could not remember the last time it had rained so much, and he was glad for his bright yellow waterproof coat. It had been ten minutes since he had shown the last children safely across the road, and he was now ready to make his way home.

Raindrops drizzled down Pops' nose, past his glasses and into his white, fluffy moustache as he trudged down the pavement, back towards Lollipop House, where Mrs Pops surely had a hot cup of tea and a teacake waiting.

Pops was everyone's friend in Middletown, and no one loved him more than the Middletown children. With his snow white hair, twinkling eyes and very tubby tummy (due to a few too many toasted teacakes), Pops really was the village character. He would show the Middletown children safely across the road every morning and every night without fail, and always with a cheery smile and a jolly joke.

Suddenly, something collided with Pops' stomach.

"Oof!" he winced, winded. Looking down, he saw what had hit him – young Amber and Jack, two of his favourite children from the school, were running home through the rain.

"Ho ho! Watch out there you two!" laughed Pops through the downpour.

"Sorry Pops," replied Amber. But Jack hadn't

heard him – the football he had been carrying was now bouncing its way across the wet road, and Jack had run straight out after it.

"Hey! Watch ou - " started Pops, but his voice was drowned out by the horn of a huge, monstrous truck, going way too fast. Pops didn't think twice; he threw down his lollipop stick, leapt out into the road, grabbed young Jack in his arms and rolled into the gutter on the other side of the road.

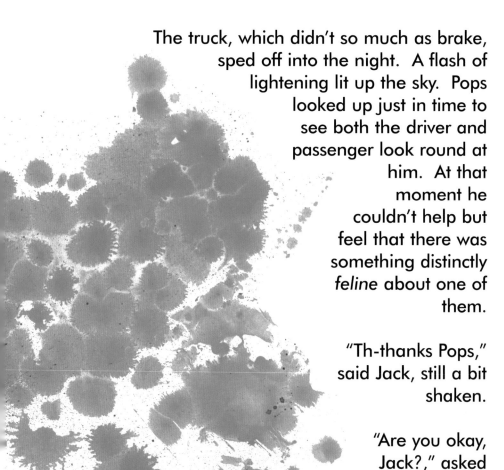

The truck, which didn't so much as brake, sped off into the night. A flash of lightening lit up the sky. Pops looked up just in time to see both the driver and passenger look round at him. At that moment he couldn't help but feel that there was something distinctly *feline* about one of them.

"Th-thanks Pops," said Jack, still a bit shaken.

"Are you okay, Jack?," asked

Amber, who had just crossed over safely, remembering to look both ways before she crossed. "Pops, you're a real hero."

"Oh, I'll never be a hero," replied Pops, as modest as ever, "From now on, just make sure you are always careful around the roads. You never know when an idiot driver like that one is about. Now, you two better run off home, you don't want to catch cold."

Amber and Jack offered to walk back with Pops, but he insisted they go straight home, so off they went.

Wet, cold and a little bruised, Pops rubbed his old back and cautiously crossed back over the road to retrieve his lollipop stick.

"I wish I knew who was driving that ~~bloomin'~~ truck" he said to himself as he crossed, "I'd teach them a lesson or two in road safety, that's for sure!"

Then, just as he reached the other side, something very strange happened. In the blink of an eye, the rain storm suddenly stopped.

'How odd!' thought Pops. He bent down to pick up the lollipop, then straightened up to look at the sky – *what was with all this peculiar weather?* But then the weather became stranger still. The clouds above Pops parted to reveal a single beam of light, which shone down on Pops like a mysterious spotlight from the heavens.

He looked up, puzzled, but not for long: he was soon distracted by a singular

fork of lightening that came hurtling towards him through the sky.

## ZAP!

The lightening struck Pops' lollipop, and sent him flying backwards onto the nearby grass.

Pops blinked, and patted himself all over to make sure he wasn't hurt. He thanked the stars that he was okay and picked himself up, thinking how lucky he was to be alive. But then, something very odd indeed began to happen. Suddenly and uncontrollably, his arm sprung into action, magically bringing the lollipop in close to his body. Then, as if it was enchanted, one leg twisted around the other, causing Pops to turn around. But he didn't stop there – his body kept turning round and he began to spin. Slowly at first, then faster and faster until he was nothing but a yellow blur. Bright stars of every colour imaginable flew off in all directions, and little forks of lightening sparked from the spinning whirl.

Eventually, the spinning began to slow, and the blur wasn't yellow anymore, but a bright, striking orange. When the spinning finally ceased, dear, simple Pops had all but disappeared. In his place stood an all-powerful **superhero**!

Pops looked down at his bright orange bodysuit and flowing yellow cape, with matching underwear pulled over the top of his tights.

Shocked at the sudden transformation, he ran over to look at his reflection in a nearby shop window, his tubby belly bouncing over the top of the yellow pants. His mouth open as wide as a manhole, Pops stared in amazement at his own face; it was now covered with a mysterious yellow-and-white mask, his unruly white moustache now neatly styled and twisted into two pointy ends.

"Oo-er!" Pops whispered to himself. His muddled old mind was confused; he really didn't know what to think. "What's all this about, eh? Oh dear, I wish Mrs Pops was here, she'd know what to do!"

No sooner had Pops spoken than his lollipop stick began to twitch in his hand. "Yeek!" squeaked Pops as the lollipop pulled at his arm. The stick was taking off into the air. Its bewildered owner hung on for dear life, his eyes shut tight.

Up and up he soared, then;

"Arrrgh!" Pops finally opened his eyes, to see a miniature Middletown below him. "Whoah! Whaoh! Stop!" he called out. The lollipop stick seemed to hear him. It climbed another few meters, then stopped sharply in midair.

"Phee-ew," sighed Pops, dangling in the sky like a ripe, round orange, ready to fall from the tree, "That's better. Now... how do I get down?"

Instantly, the lollipop stick sprung back to life, and zoomed on – this time in a downwards direction. "Yeeeeee-arrrrgh!" screamed Pops, his eyes shut again as he hurtled back down towards the houses.

It wasn't much longer, however, before he felt the stick slow down. When he opened his eyes again he saw that he was being lowered gently.

And what was beneath him? It was his very own doorstep.

# 2

Pops took a deep breath as he stood on the doorstep of his home; Lollipop House in Pee Street. Like Pops, the house in which he lived was a little unusual. You see, Pee Street is (very aptly) shaped like the letter 'P'. Consequently, it has a roundabout situated in the middle, which any passing cars have to drive around. I don't think I have to tell you where Lollipop House is built.

That's right, in the middle of this roundabout.

So, when Pops goes outside in the morning, he has to be very, very careful indeed – his front door opens straight out onto the road. This does mean, however, that Pops gets plenty of practice crossing roads safely!

LOLLIPOP HOUSE

Still stood on his doorstep, Pops was rather worried about what his wife would say about his sudden transformation. He took a deep breath, opened the door and called out.

"H-hello dear!  I'm home!"

Just finishing off her crossword in the lounge, Mrs Pops looked up to greet her husband.  She was quite taken aback at what she saw.  Instead of his usual work clothes, he was stood in the doorway, dressed like a giant tangerine in a cape, a sheepish grin spread on his face.  Luckily, Mrs Pops had a good sense of humour.

"Ho-ho!" she laughed, "You do look dashing!  What's this in aid of?"

Breathing a sigh of relief at her reaction, Pops rushed up to tell the whole amazing story.  Mrs Pops gasped and cooed in all the right places, whilst trying not to giggle at her husband's new choice in underwear.

Once he had finished his animated tale, Mrs Pops went to make a cup of tea and a toasted teacake.
Sitting there, slurping his tea and nibbling on his teacake, Pops became very thoughtful.

"Dear, I've been thinking," he said, seriously, "If I've been given these amazing powers, what do I do with them?  They could be a lot of fun, once I've got used to them, but I want to do something *worthwhile* with them .
You know, make a difference in the world."

Whilst making the tea, Mrs Pops had already decided exactly what her husband should do with his powers, but she wanted him to figure it out for himself.

"Well dear, maybe you should do something that you really believe in, something you have worked your whole life to achieve, something that will ultimately make you very happy and fulfilled."

"Hmm," thought Pops, "…you mean, I should use my powers to make the world's biggest toasted tea cake?"

Mrs Pops shook her head and smiled. Maybe she should change tactics:

"Well, try thinking about what you did just before your transformation. Perhaps you performed some sort of heroic act that meant you were chosen to become a certain type of superhero. One that is connected with your job in road safety, maybe."

Pops thought for a moment. Then, a look of revelation

appeared on his face.

"That's it! Perhaps I was chosen to become a certain *type* of superhero. One that is connected with my job in road safety!"

Mrs Pops rolled her eyes, but Pops was on a roll. He leapt up out of his seat, pointed his finger in the air, and made a confident, heartfelt speech...

"Yes, Middletown need not fear the perils of dangerous roads any longer. A new hero is in town. A hero with courage! A hero with morals! A hero with, errrm... with sound knowledge of the Green Cross Code! Together, Middletown and I will combat the villainous forces of treacherous traffic, and no more accidents need occur.

"Forget Batman! Forget Superman!"

Pops flung open the front door, kissed his wife on the cheek, and pointed his lollipop stick up at the sky.

"POPS AWAY! I'M... *LOLLIPOPMAN!*"

He pushed off the doorstep with his feet, and with a *FSHOOO!* flew off into the sky.

But he didn't get very far. Even as a superhero, Pops was still as clumsy as a dizzy octopus on stilts – he had flown straight into a telephone wire, and was now rather tangled.

"Very nice dear…" called out Mrs Pops, "You just make sure you're home in time for supper!"

Soaring through the sky, Lollipopman could see the whole of Middletown spread out beneath him. The evening rain was gone and the sun was shining brightly, meaning the Middletown children were all coming out to play. But Lollipopman wasn't there for the fun and games – he had work to do. Concerned with their safety, Lollipopman was glad of the opportunity to try out his new powers.

Down below him, Lollipopman noticed a bright red sports car driving down the Middletown main road. It was going way too fast. A determined glint in his eye, Lollipopman descended down and began flying alongside the passenger side window. Inside the car, a man in a baseball cap was listening to his booming rap music and enjoying his speedy ride. Soaring alongside, Lollipopman gave three loud knocks on the window. The startled driver's head spun round to see our moustached hero looking sternly at him and shaking his head. Perplexed, the driver pushed a button, and the car window swooshed open.

"Now, now young man," Lollipopman said, "I'm sure you're not in that much of a rush, are you?"

Mystified, the young driver flicked off his rap music and slowed right down to tortoise speed. He was now inching his way along the road.

Lollipopman smiled as a cyclist passed the stylish red sports car, ringing his bell.

**BRRING-BRRING!**

The smile didn't last long, though; Lollipopman had noticed something about the passing cyclist... he wasn't wearing a helmet!

The cyclist skidded to a halt as a big, round superhero landed in his path, his hand held up to halt the oncoming bike.

"Can, can I help you, sir?" asked the cyclist, who Lollipopman recognised as Charlie Sparrow, one of the children from Middletown School.

"No, my friend.  But maybe I can help you!  I am Lollipopman, road-crossing hero of the highways!" (Lollipopman pointed at his own head), "Now, aren't we missing something?"

"Oh, yes.  S-sorry err... Lollipop... m-man," Charlie stuttered, "I forgot to put it on.  I'm just going to my friend's house, its not far."

"Well, accidents can happen at any time, you know!  Why, only the other day I was..."

Just then, Lollipopman's stick began to twitch again. "Never mind... let's see what we can do."  He raised his lolly into the air.  It began to let out a low humming sound.  Our hapless hero didn't know what he was doing, but he was sure his magical stick wouldn't let him down.

A minute of humming passed, and nothing seemed to

happen. Charlie was looking puzzled, and Lollipopman was beginning to think he would end up looking rather foolish. Suddenly, however, something cracked up against the back of our hero's head.

"Ow!" he winced. Then he saw what was happening; Charlie's cycle helmet was now hovering above the boy. It had flown its way from the Sparrows' garage, along the streets of Middletown and was now coming safely to rest on its owner's head.

Charlie didn't know whether to be amazed by the flying helmet, or amused by Lollipopman's unfortunate bump.

"See," said Lollipopman, rubbing his head, "A knock like that can be pretty painful – but the road is much harder. Now, you'd better get going. Have fun!"

"Okay, thanks Lollipopman!" Charlie called out as he cycled safely away.

Next, Lollipopman helped the children of Marmalade Street. They had been playing cricket in the road, but

Lollipopman thought they would be much safer at the local park, and said he'd give them a lift. No sooner had he offered than his lollipop stick began to magically extend.

Longer and longer the stick stretched until it was four times as long: room enough for all the children to hang on.

"Hold on tight!" instructed Lollipopman as the gang took off into the air and soared towards the park. Once there, the children said that was much more fun than cricket and wanted to go again – but Lollipopman had work to do, so he said that they'd have to wait until the next day.

Lollipopman helped many more people that day, and was feeling very good about his new role. There was just time to help little Penny Sanderson before he had to head for home: Penny had been trying to cross the road on a nearby corner, and had been stood there for a good half hour.

Lollipopman took her up to the nearest zebra crossing.

"Okay Penny, now remember to stop and look both ways before crossing. Listen for any traffic, and then only cross when you are sure that it is safe."

Lollipopman decided that he should let Penny cross by herself, and watched as she reached the other side.

"Well done Penny. Now, take care and I'll see you tom…"

But before he could finish, a roaring truck tore over the crossing, not even slowing down to see if anyone was there. Luckily, it missed little Penny by a good metre, but bashed into a nearby parked car, leaving its front wing hanging off in a mangled mess. Lollipopman instantly recognised the truck as the same one that he had encountered earlier that day. So, after stopping off to check that Penny was okay, he raised his lollipop stick up into the air and took off in pursuit of the monstrous motor.

High up over Middletown, Lollipopman followed the smoke billowing from the back of the truck. The sun was beginning to set, and it would soon be dark. Nevertheless, Lollipopman followed the truck out of town and down a twisting road, before it stopped and disappeared under a cloud of its own smog. Lollipopman hovered for a while, waiting for the smoke to clear.

He landed cautiously and looked around. He found himself in the middle of the local scrap yard, and began to wander around. Lollipopman stared in awe: towering above him were gigantic piles of wrecked, mangled cars, stretching up into the sky and out of sight. In between the towers, hills of dented car bonnets, bent bumpers and deflated tyres completed the eerie landscape. The place was like a graveyard for unwanted vehicles and it gave our hero the creeps.

Warily, he tiptoed through the intertwining passages between the scrap piles, looking for signs of life.

Surrounded by barbed wire, an old caravan rested near to the scrap yard entrance, a number of rusted satellite dishes fastened to its side, making it look like it could topple over at any minute. A flickering blue light shone from a window. 'This must be where those two criminally careless truck drivers have disappeared to,' thought our hero.

Lollipopman sneaked up to the caravan and stepped onto a car tyre to secretly spy through the window. Inside, two villains were hatching a wicked plan...

"Curses!" grunted a large man in a string vest, pyjama bottoms and slippers, taking a sip from a can of beer, "Out driving at lightening fast speeds in the middle of a rain storm, and barely a single accident caused! I'll get more car wrecks for my scrap heap, or my name's not Scrappy Joe!"

POLICE DEPT.
JOE, SCRAPPY
209946

Lollipopman had heard a little bit about Scrappy Joe, although he was not well known in Middletown. Joe preferred to keep himself to himself, and what he liked doing with himself most of all was watching television. He would sit in his armchair and watch television night and day, day and night. It didn't matter what was on - so long as no-one onscreen said any long words, he'd happily watch whatever flashed before his eyes.

At the far end of the caravan, Lollipopman noticed where the flickering blue light was coming from. Covering *half* of the far wall, a massive TV set was blaring out a ridiculous theme tune even as Scrappy Joe spoke.

"One day soon, I'll have sold enough scrap to afford a TV that covers the *whole* of the wall – and even get one of them new, fangled digi-boxes to go with it! Isn't that right, my precious scrap guard?"

Now, if you've ever passed a scrap yard you'll have noticed that most of them have guard dogs. You can't so much as tiptoe past the gate of a scrap yard without some mongrel barking and slathering at you as if you were made of Meaty Chunks dog food. But not in Middletown. No, the Middletown scrap yard had something much, much worse than a guard dog – the most ferocious cat you'll ever see!

He was called Fat Cat, and he was (as you might have guessed from his name) rather large. So large, in fact, that Scrappy Joe's cat flap takes up more than half of his caravan door! Not only was Fat Cat the size of a baby elephant, he also had the most horribly matted fur, the sharpest claws, and the most vicious teeth you'll ever see.

Fat Cat's purr sounded like a rumbling, angry lawnmower, hungry for grass. His meow was so high-pitched, it made you want to scrape your fingernails down the nearest blackboard just to drown out the sound.

He also had only the one eye. The other one had been scratched out in a cat fight. Fat Cat, of course, got his revenge by sitting on the culprit – and soon replaced his missing eye with one of those little reflective contraptions from the middle of the road. They don't call them 'cats eyes' for nothing!

So, all in all, Fat Cat was so much more effective at scaring people away from the Middletown scrap yard than any dog!

Incidentally, Scrappy Joe did once buy a guard-dog. The dog's name was Brute and he was a monster of a mongrel, with muscles like bricks and jaws as ravenous as a piranha on a diet. Scrappy Joe bought Brute one Christmas after some local children had interrupted his favourite show, 'When Monster Trucks Attack', with their tuneful carol singing. Brute's job was to bite the knees of anyone even whispering the words "Merry Christmas".

Brute lasted just under a week.

Within that time, Fat Cat had scratched his nose, bitten his ear, and clawed at his tail. At night, Fat Cat would sit and glare at Brute, with his glowing yellow eyes, making the poor dog afraid to even think about going to sleep. Fat Cat even did something rather unpleasant in Brute's bowl of dog food (the less said about that, the better).

In fact, Fat Cat tormented the poor beast so much, that after six days Brute had gone completely round the bend.

Brute now lives with three poodles at Scrappy Joe's gran's house. She dresses him up in pink bows and a fluffy lilac bonnet like a big sissy-dog. No one can threaten Fat Cat's rule of the scrap yard.

And what a rule it was, for in the folds and crannies of the towering blocks of car wrecks lived Fat Cat's servants: every freak and villain for miles around.

For example, in a battered old burger van lived three ugly, crooked old ladies known as the T-Bags. Underneath a mound of discarded car tyres resided a mysterious and sinister white rabbit. The rest of the yard was over-run by three thousand dirty rats.

These rats had become very good at fashioning contraptions and gadgets from the pieces of scrap discarded in the yard. Each of their tiny homes featured appliances made from bits and pieces of crashed cars; miniature sofas made from arm rests, cookers made from cigarette lighters, and working lights fashioned from headlamps. These rubbish-dwelling rascals would do whatever Fat Cat commanded. If they didn't, he'd simply gobble them up for breakfast.

Outside the caravan, Lollipopman listened carefully through the window. Scrappy Joe had been distracted for a while by an advert warning against the dangers of drink driving (which he found *very* funny), but now he was in full flow, revealing his new plan to his plump pet.

"Okay, my treasure, here's the plan," growled Scrappy Joe, "You get your scrap yard slaves to cause as many accidents as they can. We'll collect all the scrap cars, strip them for parts, and sell them for oodles of lovely cash. Then I'll be able to afford the TV of my dreams – and you, my bonny little bundle of blubber, will be the king of the biggest catty kingdom for miles around."

With that, Scrappy Joe leant back in his armchair, pointed the remote control at the TV, and turned the volume up as high as it would go. Fat Cat curled up by his side, and shut his eye, a wide smirk curling up his lips.

Outside, Lollipopman shook his head. Then his expression changed from one of despair to determination - he would now work doubly hard to protect the people of Middletown against this devishly devious plot. He raised his lollipop into the air and blasted off for home.

Several weeks had past since Pops' first transformation into Lollipopman. In the time since then, he had managed to stop almost every car accident in Middletown, and was passing on his 'road-safety-style' to everyone around. In fact, Lollipopman had become quite a celebrity, his heroics appearing on the front page in the local newspaper just about every day.

Nobody had guessed, however, that this

*Middletown ✠ Gazette*

# WHO IS THIS MASKED MAN?

**Superhero saves town!**

Blah blah blah, waffle waffle waffle, same old same old, yap yap yap.

"Blabber blabber blabber" says man. "Rabbit rabbit rabbit" says woman. "Baa baa baa" says sheep.

Gobbledy gook, jam sandwich, flim flam, flim flam, drivel drivel, blah blah, load of old flannel.

Ooh ah-ah. Wolla wolla bing bong. I want chicken I want liver - Meow-mix meow-mix please deliver!

Editor sacked for writing nonsense. See page 14.

mysterious masked man was really none other than Pops, Middletown's sweet, old lollipop man.

Today was Friday, and Pops was in his usual spot. Even though he was now a secret superhero, and the most famous person in town, Pops didn't want to give up his very important job of showing the local children safely across the busy road to school. He loved his job, and he loved seeing the happy faces of the Middletown children every morning.

As this week had gone on, however, the children's faces had seemed to be getting a little less happy each day. Today, in fact, they all looked positively miserable – it didn't

even raise a smirk when Pops accidentally knocked off his own hat with his stick, then tore his trousers when he bent down to pick it up. This was most unusual, and Pops decided it was about time he got to the bottom of these strange goings-on. When his two favourite children, Amber and Jack, arrived, he greeted them with his usual cheery smile and twinkling eyes.

"Good morning, kids! Oh my – you two look like you've just pulled open a bag of sweets and found it's full of soggy sprouts! What's wrong with everyone this week?"

"You're not far off with the sprouts, actually, Pops," answered Amber, "We're dreading lunchtime – some new dinner ladies have joined the school, and their food's horrible!"

"That's right" added Jack, "Cold chips, rancid sausages, peas like gravel. I can't even stomach the pudding," (and Jack loved pudding) "The custard's so lumpy, you can't tell what's pudding and what's lump!"

Pops shook his head and smoothed his silvery-white eyebrows with concern.

"New dinner ladies, eh? School dinners not up to scratch? Hmm, that'll never do. Never do."

Stood in the middle of the road, Pops' thoughts were interrupted by an annoyed driver on his way to work, beeping his horn impatiently.

"You kids better get going. Take care now," called out Pops as they reached the other side of the road, "You don't want to be late for class!"

"I wouldn't mind!" whispered Jack to his sister as they left Pops behind, "At least Pops doesn't have to put up with old Mr Crumbweasel!"  Little did they know, however, that today Pops would face a far greater foe.

Standing at the side of the road with his lollipop, Pops waited until the last of the children were in school and out of sight, then whispered to himself.

"Hmm, grotty school dinner, eh?  We can't have that!  This looks like a job for…"

He checked to see no one was around, brought his lollipop stick in close to his body, twisted one leg around the other and began to spin into a yellow and white blur.

### *"…Lollipopman!"*

With a smile as broad as a zebra crossing, Lollipopman lifted his lollipop stick into the air, and with a whoosh he flew off into the clouds.

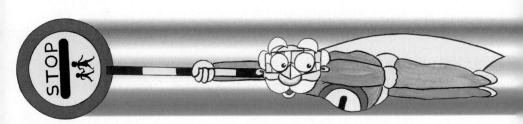

In the Middletown school kitchen, three dingy, dirty dinnerladies were cooking up a dastardly mess for the children's dinner.

The dinnerladies all looked very different, but equally disgusting. The first was as tall and slender as a stick insect, her face caked in make-up in a vain attempt to cover up her ugliness. The second had a hunched back, squinty eyes and a hooked nose, making her look distinctly like a vile vulture. The third was as short and round as a beach ball, only with a cigarette stuck out of the side.

"Hmmm," said Stick Insect, taking a sip from a steaming vat of gravy, "Needs a little something else..."

Beach Ball took the cigarette out of her mouth, and tapped the ash into the gravy. She reached up to a nearby shelf, lifted down a tall aerosol can, and sprayed it into the gravy.

"Heh-heh!" she cackled, "The finest fly spray - made with 100% fly!"

"Excellent!" sneered the Vile Vulture, sampling the gravy again, "Now for the finishing touch!"

She peeled a sticking plaster from her finger, and dropped it into the steaming mixture. She stirred the gravy with a giant ladle.

"Grrmm," she moaned, "It's not quite thick enough!"

She picked up a potted spider plant from the nearby window sill, pulled the plant out with one hand and was ready to empty the soil from the pot into the slimy brown goo, when she was distracted. The three dodgy dinnerladies spun round as the back door to the kitchen burst open.

Silhouetted in the doorway was Lollipopman, his cape flapping in the wind. The dinnerladies gasped.

"Well, well, well!" bellowed Lollipopman, "If it isn't the T-Bags! I thought as much – Fat Cat sent you, did he? Well, are you going to come quietly?"

"Not a chance!" yelled Vile Vulture, "*Wally*-pop Man!"

With that, she grabbed a nearby ladle, and catapulted a mouldy mass of mushy peas in Lollipopman's direction. Without battering an eyelid, he jammed his stick against the floor and pole-vaulted out of the way. The grubby green grenades splattered harmlessly against the windows and walls.

"Ha ha!" laughed Lollipopman, "That the best you got?"

"We've only just begun!" shrieked Beach Ball, producing a platter of rock-solid currant buns. The T-Bags began flinging them at Lollipopman.

He quickly threw forward his lollipop so that he was holding it at the very end, then tapped the round end on the ground three times.

"Good job I was good at cricket when I was a lad, eh?" he quipped, as he expertly knocked the currant buns for six.

One bun went soaring through the air and hit a biscuit-tin on a top kitchen unit. The biscuit-tin fell over onto its side, and rolled along the shelf.

Lollipopman, meanwhile, was still batting the rock cakes back as quickly as the T-Bags could throw them. "Ho-ho!" he laughed, "Even your worst cooking can't stop this crossing crusader!"

Meanwhile, the biscuit-tin was continuing its long journey across the shelf. It came to a sudden halt when it hit a saltcellar, causing the biscuit-tin lid to fall off.

The rock cakes were coming quicker and harder now and Lollipopman was getting flustered. He ducked as one zoomed past his ear – a little too close for comfort!

Out of the biscuit tin rolled a cascade of stale biscuity boulders, which fell to the floor with a series of thuds. One biscuit landed very precisely on the pedal of the pedal bin.

As the bin flew open, a discarded tea-bag was catapulted off the lid and tore through the air.

The T-Bags were now throwing the rock cakes at an extraordinary rate. Lollipopman wasn't so much knocking them back, as using his lollipop to guard his face, the clang of each incoming rock cake making him wince horribly.

The flying tea bag splattered against the kitchen window, making it swing open. A sudden gust of wind blew through, setting a nearby rolling-pin tumbling off the worktop and across the kitchen floor.

"Haw-haw!" sniggered Stick Insect, as she threw a particularly large rock cake, "This'll end your road-crossin' days!"

In a rather silly move, Lollipopman popped his head out

from behind the lollipop to see what she was talking about, just in time to see a massive rock cake before it bashed him on the head and knocked him out cold.

"Let's get 'im!" called out Beach Ball, ready to race towards the poor, unconscious Lollipopman.

"Whooooooooah!" she screamed, as she stepped on the rolling rolling-pin and went somersaulting into the air.

The other two T-Bags looked on in horror as Beach Ball came crashing down onto the edge of the gravy vat, causing a tidal wave of gooey, gluey gravy to cascade over all three dinnerladies, covering them from head to foot.

At the far end of the kitchen, Lollipopman started to come round. Rubbing his head, he looked over to see the three T-Bags completely stuck together in a messy, sticky heap.

"Oh, errr… Ha ha!" he laughed, a little baffled as to how he had triumphed.  "Erm, yes… That'll teach you to mess with Pop… I mean, Lollipopman!"

Our lucky hero took the end of a strand of super-rubbery spaghetti from a nearby pot and, holding his lollipop before him, he flew circles round the T-Bags until they were completely tied together.

"Now to sort out those scrap yard scoundrels!"

Lollipopman raised his lolly into the air and flew off through the skylight, swinging the T-Bags behind him like a giant conker.

Two scrawny rats clambered up onto a majestic throne made of bits and pieces of compressed cars and motorbikes. Between them, they carried a discarded car aerial, on which they had threaded a few pieces of rotten fruit and mouldy meat, just like a kebab. They scurried onto the throne and trudged over the colossal furry belly which was slumped there, until they came to an open mouth full of razor-sharp teeth. They stopped, one on either side of the mouth, and placed the kebab between the jaws. The rats spun the kebab round as the jaws closed around it, and in no time at all the food was gone.

As quickly as they could, the rats scurried back down the belly, and vanished into the rubbish.

Another rat appeared, this time with a piece of material torn from a car seat. It wiped the scraps of food from around the wide, purring mouth. It was about to scamper away again, when it was swept off its feet by a long, powerful tail. The rat went flying into the air. The tail hit it again, in midair, and the rat

K1NG

disappeared into the cavernous mouth.

Fat Cat gulped.

"*BURP!* …You missed a spot!" he sneered to the chewed-up rat in his belly.

With ripples of blubber making his limbs barely visible, Fat Cat was as big as a boulder. He was still able, however, to slowly pull himself upright in his throne. He closed his eyes, raised his head, and let out a cringe-inducing, meowing scream.

At this, a thousand rats appeared from the hidden pockets of the scrap heap, and stared in Fat Cat's direction. After a long moment of tense silence, Fat Cat opened his eyelids to reveal both his real and spooky artificial eye. They emanated a yellow glow, as if a candle had been lit behind them.

"My loyal servants! Our magnificent city, built from the finest scrap in the country, has been our home for many glorious years. But I have a vision of ruling the biggest kingdom a cat has ever ruled. I can only achieve this with more car wrecks, more motorbike remains, and more discarded lorry parts.

"So far, however, we have tried in vain to create more road accidents. And all this is down to one man! The high ruler of road safety himself – *Lollipopman*! But thanks to my fiendishly clever plan, today we will capture the old fool. I knew that so-called superhero wouldn't be able to see those school brats unhappy… the T-Bags were bait, and he took it, like the pathetic little rodent he is!

"He is expected any minute now, so be ready!  With Lollipopman out of the way, we will be able to create enough road chaos to make *Catifornia* the biggest city in the world!"

The rats squeaked with excitement as they darted off in different directions to prepare for Lollipopman's arrival.

Soaring above the clouds with the T-Bags bouncing along behind him, Lollipopman spotted the scrap yard below.

"Hold onto your wigs!" he called to them as he began his descent.

Lollipopman knew instantly what to do with the T-Bags. He headed straight for the scrap yard's crane, and left the phoney dinnerladies dangling high above the yard by the straps of their spaghetti straight jacket, struggling to get free.

With a whoosh, the superhero landed in a clearing. He spotted Fat Cat in the distance. The porky puss had spent the day plucking cats eyes from the middle of the road (he always liked to keep spares), and was now relaxing on his scrap throne, dreaming of all the accidents this might cause.

"Hand over the real school dinnerladies, you mangy moggy!"

Fat Cat snapped out of his daydream and leapt up in

surprise.

"Never!" Fat Cat screeched back, waving his fist in the air, "You'll have to get through me first!"

Lollipopman raced towards Fat Cat, but the rascally rats blocked his path. At either side of him, bursts of flame exploded from overturned, discarded cookers.

"Crikey!" yelled Lollipopman, trying to turn back, but instead tripping over his own feet and tumbling over. Luckily, this meant that he rolled underneath the first fire-burst – his clumsiness could be useful sometimes.

He soon found his feet again, only to find a second fireball bursting in front of him. The flame was lower this time, so Lollipopman used his lollipop to propel himself over the top.

A third flame erupted in front of Lollipopman's face, and he was just quick enough to lean right back, the fire just missing his nose.

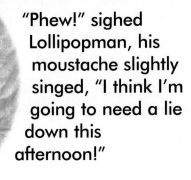

"Phew!" sighed Lollipopman, his moustache slightly singed, "I think I'm going to need a lie down this afternoon!"

Rubbing his back, Lollipopman spotted Fat Cat again and continued on his way. But he didn't get far.

Fat Cat was trudging off behind his car wreck throne and towards a huge mountain of scrap. Lollipopman began to run in the same direction, but was distracted by a high-pitched squeak coming from his left. He spun round just in time to see a line of rats running towards him with a rusty pipe raised above their heads, a sharpened windscreen wiper fastened to the end.

Lollipopman thought quickly. He pulled his hat out from under his cape and skimmed it through the air like a frisbee, hoping to knock the rats off their feet. At the last minute, though, he clumsily trod on his own cape and tripped, head over heels.

"Whooooooaah... oof!"

The hat missed the rats by a long shot, and went soaring high into the air. The rats sniggered as they raced towards the fallen hero, who was struggling to free himself from his tangled cape.

High above them, however, the T-Bags were still swinging from the crane. The terrible trio let out a warped scream as Lollipopman's hat sliced through the line of spaghetti. The sticky gravy boulder plummeted through the air, landing squarely on top of the line of rats with a clattering crash.

Lollipopman finally untangled himself from the cape, to see the T-Bags groaning in a heap on the floor.

"Oh, sorry ladies – all in the line of duty!"

With the rats out of the way, Lollipopman finally caught up with Fat Cat as he reached the bottom of the scrap mountain.

"Curse you, Lollipopman!" shouted the cat, as he struggled to pull himself up a pile of rubbish next to a battered old ice-cream van. Sticking his head out of the driver's window of the van, Scrappy Joe shouted at his feline partner in crime. After hearing the commotion outside, he had finally emerged from his TV den to sort things out for himself.

"You stupid cat!" Joe yelled, "Do I have to do everything myself? Tearing me away from my TV programme: you're lucky it's the ad break! Well, what are you waiting for?" he pointed to the ice-cream van roof, "You know your place!"

Fat Cat struggled onto the ice-cream van roof. Here, the scrap yard rats had fashioned a sling shot from a discarded pair of frilly knickers, stretched between the two speakers at the front of the van roof. Fat Cat bounced across the roof to the sling shot.

He let out a meowing signal, and a flurry of rats spilled out of the surrounding scrap and into the van.

Lollipopman watched in puzzlement as the engine started up, the glass serving hatch slid open and the tune of *Humpty Dumpty* chimed out from the old ice-cream van. Scrappy Joe put his foot down and the van trundled forward, choking black smoke from its exhaust pipe as it went.

A gaggle of rats had formed a line, stretching from the ice-cream dispensing machine, through the open serving hatch and up onto the roof. As the old van rattled towards Lollipopman, the rats were whipping up cornets from the dispenser and passing them along the line to Fat Cat, up on the roof.

Fat Cat placed the ice cream cone into the frilly knickers, and pulled them back as far as they would go. He let go, and fired the first ice-cream missile at Lollipopman, who had only just figured out what was going on. The cold cornet splattered against the side of our hero's face. He managed to wipe it off, only for a second cone to splodge against his stomach, then a third – and a forth.

The missiles were coming thick and fast from the approaching van. Lollipopman managed to use his lollipop stick to block them for a while, but they were coming too hard and too fast. Suddenly, one hit the lollipop so hard that it was knocked clean out of our hero's hands.

Inside, Scrappy Joe laughed manically above the musical chime of the van. Fat Cat cackled, the piercingly cold ice-creams pounding into Lollipopman's face as he bent down to fumble for his missing shield. But it was too difficult, with the van fast approaching, and the bombarding cornets getting ever more painful, he had no choice but to turn and run away from the chiming van.

With the shower of ice-cold cornets hammering into his back, Lollipopman scrambled up the mountain of scrap in the hope of shaking off the dastardly duo. Up and up he climbed, but the old van must have been tougher than it looked, for it managed to clatter slowly up the bank of bent metal, its musical melody still chiming happily.

Higher and higher he climbed until, huffing and puffing, Lollipopman reached the top of the mountain of scrap. He screeched to a halt as he saw what was on the other side. A bent bicycle wheel fell away from under the superhero's feet, and plunged straight down a sheer cliff face of rubbish. The wheel disappeared out of sight, quickly followed by a crash of metal and a cloud of dust far below. Lollipopman gulped, and turned around to step away from the edge.

# SPLAT!

An ice cream cone struck him in the nose. The approaching van was halfway up the scrap mountain. Lollipopman was cornered.

Fat Cat saw our hero's hopeless situation, and let out a menacing guffaw. With Lollipopman gone, there would be no one to stop Fat Cat and Scrappy Joe causing as many nasty accidents as they could manage. At this evil thought, Fat Cat began to sing his own taunt along with van's ding-dong version of Humpty Dumpty…

*"Stupid, brainless*
*Lollipopman,*
*Thinks he can*
*Foil our plan.*

*Say goodbye, kids,*
*To your road-crossing friend.*
*Your days of safety,*
*Have come to an end!"*

Fat Cat sniggered at his own skit, but in front of him, Lollipopman was seeing red: it was one thing to mess with him, but to threaten the safety of the children was another. With this thought in his head, Lollipopman was unstoppable. Glaring straight at Fat Cat, he marched toward the looming van. The ice-cream missiles battered against his body as he approached, but with his new-found determination, our hero pressed on, ignoring the onslaught.

Suddenly the cornet missiles ceased. Fat Cat was beginning to fret. And for good reason, as Lollipopman was in front of the van now and was taking a run-up. He stepped up onto the front bumper and onto the bonnet. Scrappy Joe looked on in wonder as our hero ran up the windshield and leapt over Fat Cat's head and onto the roof. Fat Cat spun round to see Lollipopman, fists clenched, stepping towards him. Panicking, the feline stumbled backwards, not seeing what was behind him.

"Yeeek!" he yelped, tangling himself up in the sling shot.

The angry look in Lollipopman's face quickly disappeared as he was confronted with his arch enemy struggling to get out of a pair of frilly, pink knickers.

"Ho-ho!" he chuckled, "Looks like this is going to be easier than I thought."

He pulled the knickers back with his finger, stretching them as far as they would go, and…

## TWANG!

Inside the ice-cream van, Scrappy Joe watched as his pet went flying over the edge of scrap

heap mountain and

# SPLODGE!

landed head-first in a barrel of grease. Back in the van, the rats looked at each other in fright, and in a split second they had scarpered through the window and back into the folds of the scrap yard.

The ice-cream van, however, continued to rattle and shake up the scrap mountain. Scrappy Joe was determined to shake off his foe for good. Up on the roof, Lollipopman saw the vast drop approaching again.

He gulped. Holding on tight, he swung himself off the roof, down through the open serving-hatch and into the van. He dashed into the cockpit and was

confronted with the angry scrap yard owner. Letting go of the steering wheel, Scrappy Joe grabbed hold of Lollipopman's collar.

"You just can't stop meddling, can you old man? If you think I'm going to let a buffoon in tights wreck my TV dreams, you've got another thing coming! Well, I'm gonna punch your traffic lights out, mate. Say goodnight, you superzero!"

At that moment Lollipopman spotted the only thing that could save him now; Scrappy Joe's remote control was hanging out of his pocket.

"Sorry, I can't say goodnight," Lollipopman replied, "It's not my afternoon nap time for another hour!" He swiped the remote control out of Joe's pocket, and threw it out of the open window.

"My baby!" shrieked Scrappy Joe. He promptly flung open the ice-cream van door, and leapt out to retrieve his most precious gizmo.

With Scrappy Joe gone, Lollipopman was free to stop the van. He fumbled with the key to switch off the engine. The ice-cream van came to a slow, shaky stop, the chiming music winding down to a slow slur. Then, silence.

Slumped in the driving seat, Lollipopman breathed a sigh of relief – the van had stopped right on the brink of the canyon edge, rocking slightly but just secure. Through the window, he looked out over the cliff edge and across the scrap yard. The midday sun was high above him, and in the distance he could see Middletown. He sat and gazed at his bungalow, in the middle of the roundabout in Pee Street, the windows open to let in the midday breeze. He thought of Mrs Pops – she would just be getting ready to make his lunch right now. Lollipopman's stomach rumbled.

'I can't think about my stomach now,' he thought to himself, 'I've still got work to do. We can't have the children going hungry – I must find the real school dinnerladies before its too late.'

His stomach rumbled again. Only this time it was so loud that all the birds in the distant trees all took flight at once.

'Oh well,' thought our hungry hero, 'I shouldn't work on an empty stomach, should I?'

Climbing into the back of the ice-cream van, Lollipopman flung open the freezer lid in the hope of finding a left-over choc ice. But instead, he leapt back in surprise at what he saw: the real dinnerladies, Mo, Flo and old Mrs Snow, shivering with cold.

"M-my goodness, are you a sight for sore eyes!" stammered Mo.

"Why, yes - we were afraid we were going to perish in here!" exclaimed Flo.

~~"Ooh - isn't 'e 'andsome!" added old Mrs Snow.~~

~~Lollipopman blushed, but Mrs Snow carried on.~~

"How clever of you to know exactly where that naughty cat

and his smelly owner had hidden us,"

"Oh, err... y-yes!" stuttered Lollipopman, not wanting to reveal the real reason why he had stumbled across the three, "I mean, where else could you have been?  Now," (he quickly changed the subject), "Its nearly lunchtime, we'd better get you three back to the school, eh?  This adventure isn't quite over yet - we can't have those children going hungry now, can we?  No, just one last lollipop flight - I'd better find my faithful stick!"

He lifted them out of the freezer, one by one, and climbed out of the van to try and find his lolly.

But he needn't have looked far.  Further down the scrap mountain stood Scrappy Joe, the magic lollipop stick firmly in his great, hairy hands.

"Ha ha!  Not so clever now, are we Lollipopman?  Just think of the accidents I can cause with this; the money'll be rolling in!"  Scrappy Joe's eyes almost lit up at the greedy thought, "But before that, it's time to settle a few scores.  Say goodbye to your girlfriends – they won't think you're as attractive when you're at the bottom of that canyon!"

With that, Scrappy Joe pointed the lollipop stick up the mountain and lined up his round, orange target.  Joe pushed off with his feet and went flying towards our hero, a murderous look in his eye.  All Lollipopman could do was close his eyes, as the scruffy scoundrel came hurtling in his direction to push him into oblivion.

But, as you will remember, Lollipopman's stick is a very magical stick indeed, and instead of taking Scrappy Joe all the way to our hero, it veered off to the side, and began to climb higher and higher into the sky. Joe hollered in fright as the stick took him up into the clouds and began to dart backwards and forwards at a terrifying rate.

Next it swivelled in a figure of eight, before jerking downwards and began to plunge towards the ground. Scrappy Joe was white with fright now as the scrap yard beneath him advanced at a startling pace. But just as it was about to hit the ground, the lollipop stick jerked back up again. Joe couldn't hold on, and his hand was torn away, leaving him free-falling through the air.

Back on the ground, Fat Cat had finally managed to struggle his way to the top of the barrel of oil, and was about to pull himself out, when;

# SPLATTER!

His beefy boss landed right on his head, sending them both plunging into the dirty sludge.

Up on top of the scrap mountain, Lollipopman and the three dinnerladies laughed as the two villains strained to pull themselves out of the tight, oily barrel. The struggling caused the barrel to fall onto its side, and the last Lollipopman saw, it was rolling down the hill and out of sight.

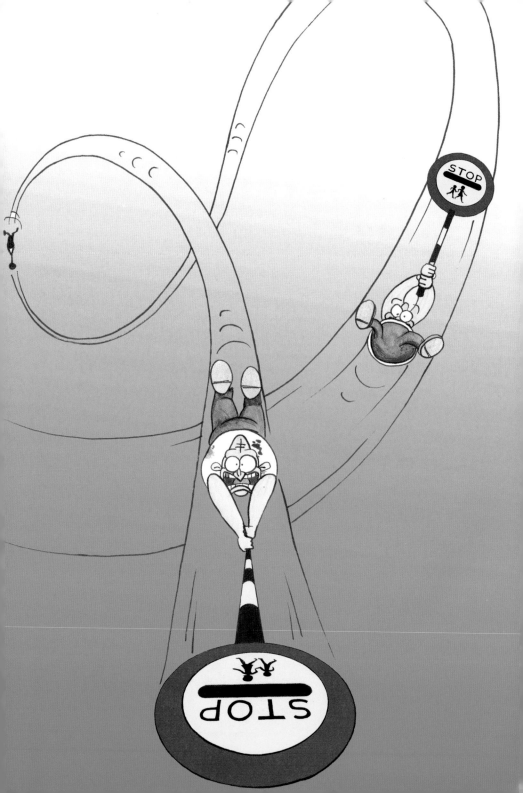

By now, the lollipop stick had flown its way up to its rightful owner.

"Okay ladies," said a triumphant Lollipopman, "Hold on tight. This shouldn't take long!"

It was the end of the school day, and Amber and Jack raced down the street, excited to get home and play. They screeched to a halt at the side of the road, and waited patiently for Pops to wave them over.

"How was your day, kids?" asked Pops, a gleaming smile on his face.

"Brilliant, thanks, Pops!

Dinner was yummy!" chirped Amber.

"We even got seconds of treacle pud!" added Jack.

"And we didn't get any homework from Crumbweasel!" said Amber, excitedly as they all crossed the road. She continued; "So what did you get up to today Pops?"

"Bet you've been napping since we left you, eh?" asked Jack, rather cheekily, as the two reached the other side.

"Ho ho!" laughed Pops, "Not at all, kids – I've been off saving the world from the clutches of evil!"

"Sounds like a dream to me, Pops!" chuckled Amber

"Maybe it was kids, maybe it was!" Pops called after them, as the pair headed for home.

Pops smiled to himself, and began to wonder what Mrs Pops would rustle up for them to eat that evening. Before he could decide, however, he heard the distinctive whimper of a hedgehog trying to cross the road three miles away.

The white-haired old man looked around to check that no one was watching. He brought his lollipop stick in close to his body, twisted one leg around the other and began to spin...

# BE A HERO... WITH LOLLIPOPMAN!

*Follow these rules and you too can beat the perils of traffic:*

**Follow the Green Cross Code, always STOP, LOOK and LISTEN before crossing roads.**

**Always wear a cycle helmet when cycling - it could save your life.**

**Always wear a seat belt when travelling by car.**

**Wear something bright and reflective when out and about at night or in poor weather.**

Brake
the road safety charity
www.brake.org.uk

# COMING SOON

## Lollipopman and the Rabbit of Doom

The Middletown children are acting very strangely indeed – crossing the road without looking, walking across backwards, and even doing chicken impressions!

So, it's our hapless hero Lollipopman to the rescue! Going undercover in various disguises at the school, Lollipopman soon reveals the culprit – the school pet rabbit is hypnotising the children.

Now, the race is on the stop Hypnobunny causing any more accidents.

# COMING SOON

## Lollipopman and the War of the Rats

Chaos hits Middletown. With traffic cones falling from lampposts, road signs disappearing up trees, and traffic lights flashing like a disco, the roads are more dangerous than ever. What is more, all the country's lollipop people have gone missing!

With Lollipopman facing his greatest challenge yet, he needs a little help from his friends – including the magical road sign folk and lollipop people from around the world,

As the Lollipop Trilogy comes to thrilling end, will Lollipopman foil his foes' plans for good, or will he come to a very sticky end?

# About the Author

Born in 1980, Philip Sheppard's Edinburgh Fringe show, *Ever After*, received rave reviews:

*"Professional quality cartoons and impressive impersonations... clever gags and word play permeate the script..."*
**(Edinburgh Guide)**

*"...a fantastic achievement that is truly enjoyable."*

**(Three Weeks magazine)**

The Lollipop Trilogy is his first series of books.
E-mail him on phil@lollipopman.co.uk